You Are Music

Trila N. Malone

ISBN 978-1-63903-807-7 (paperback)
ISBN 978-1-63903-808-4 (digital)

Christian Faith Publishing
832 Park Avenue
Meadville, PA 16335
www.christianfaithpublishing.com

Printed in the United States of America

This book is dedicated to my five children who all remind me of music. They are all individual songs that compel my very soul. Their lives are playing out in such a fashion that draws me in continuously. They are comically dramatic, joyously intrinsic, and beautifully compelling in every way. They are compassionate and passionate about their family and friends as well as their individual arts and talents. They are the best parts of me.

Before I ever saw you, I heard you. The quick beats of your heart were a rhythmic sound that gave me chills.

When I first saw you on the ultrasound machine, you swam in my tummy like a dance. I felt a rush just to know you were so tiny and there, so cozy and content.

When you were born, I held my breath until I heard your first cry; and when I heard your little voice, it was music to my ears. You are music.

Your first words sounded like music.

When I put my ear to your little chest, your heartbeat was like the sound of the drums playing a tune.

Your first laugh was musical. Even your little hiccups were a pleasant sound. You are music.

So it doesn't surprise me that you love the sound of music.

You are writing lyrics to every beat. With every sound, you move your feet.

You dance in such complicated moves. You move to the beat. You cruise to the groove. You say you need music to start your day. You cannot stand the quiet; it darkens your way.

If you are ever lonely, the lyrics always play to your favorite song and keep you at bay.

Music is like every breath you take. You are composing when you are sleeping, and you are writing when you are awake.

You love music, and music loves you. It is a part of your life and everything you do.

As you walk down the street, everything turns into a tune, from the rustling leaves to the flowers that bloom. From the singing birds to the swaying trees, you see everything music, and it makes your life gleam.

So spread your wings like the birds that fly. Let nothing stop you. Never ask yourself why. Just know before you were even born, you were sweet music, and now you are my song.

About the Author

Trila Naomie Malone was born on the West Side, the blessed side, of Chicago. She is the fifth child of seven children. She is a mother of five children: one girl and four boys. She has one grandson and a shih tzu–Maltese pup.

But her life, her story, carries so much more weight and depth than you can ever imagine. They say that diamonds are made in the roughest, toughest environments. *You Are Music* is the result of Trila channeling every one of life's obstacles thus far and turning them into pure gold.

Trila is an avid writer, a wonderful mother, and a nurturer in the Twin Cities. *You Are Music* is the first of many books and stories to come. When she isn't writing, she is enjoying life and learning to find beauty in every tiny detail.

CPSIA information can be obtained
at www.ICGtesting.com
Printed in the USA
BVHW010851010323
659464BV00015B/581

9 781639 038077